D0412422

ON PLANET
FRUITCAKE

ON PLANET FRUITCAKE

ANNE FINE

Illustrated by Kate Aldous

EGMONT

You can visit Anne Fine's website
www.annefine.co.uk

and download free bookplates from
www.myhomelibrary.org

EGMONT
We bring stories to life

First published in Great Britain 2013
This edition published 2018
by Egmont UK Limited
The Yellow Building, 1 Nicholas Road, London W11 4AN

Text copyright © Anne Fine 2013
Illustrations copyright © Kate Aldous 2013

The moral rights of the author and illustrator have been asserted

ISBN 978 1 4052 8899 6

52056/5

A CIP catalogue record for this title is available from the British Library

Typeset by Avon DataSet Ltd, Bidford on Avon, Warwickshire
Printed and bound in Great Britain by the CPI Group

For Kit, of course.

Contents

Problem!

Poor Philip had a problem. Everyone else adored his teacher, Miss Dove. They thought she was the nicest, kindest teacher in the whole school.

'We are so *lucky* that we're in her class!' Beth kept on telling everyone.

'Yes,' Peter agreed. 'She never gives us vinegary looks, the way the janitor does when we come in on wet mornings, tracking mud all over his clean floors.'

'Or makes her mouth go tight and crimpy, like Mrs Edmond does when she's getting ratty.'

Philip said nothing, but he wasn't so sure.

1

He liked Miss Dove. Of course he did. She was so gentle. But every time she called him up to her desk for a private chat, she said the very same thing.

'Philip, you're always so quiet when we have class discussions. You never put up your hand to tell us what you think. Do you suppose you might be a little *shy*?'

Poor Philip always shrugged. He didn't believe he was shy. He made as much noise as anyone else in the playground. He cheered as loudly as everyone else when he heard there was pizza for lunch.

But he was quiet in class. He couldn't think of anything he really wanted to say. If Miss Dove asked him a question like, 'Does metal float?', or, 'What are seven threes?', he answered quickly enough. But when they talked about things in class, Philip could never think of anything to add to what the others had all said already.

So he was quiet. What was wrong with that?

Beth was still going on about how lucky they were. 'Miss Dove never snaps at us like Mr Huggett does when he catches us mucking about in the corridors.'

'No,' Astrid said. 'And her eyes never go all narrow, like a cat's, and flash the scary way Miss Gelland's do if you forget your sports stuff.'

Still Philip said nothing. He was remembering the last time his mum and dad came back from meeting Miss Dove on parents' evening.

'She says you're very quiet in class,' his mum had told him.

'Too quiet,' said his dad. 'She says you don't join in the class discussions. Why is that, Philip? Are you a little scared of her?'

Scared of Miss Dove? How could you *ever* be scared of Miss Dove. She never made them jump by hissing at them to be quiet, like Mr Pound. Or gave them really fierce looks, like Mrs Carter did if ever they whispered in Assembly. She was the nicest teacher he'd ever had.

Still, on his end of term report she'd written, *Philip must try to make more of an effort to speak up in class discussions.*

Not that it was easy to get a word in edgeways with his class. Someone was always talking. Even now, James was giving everyone another reason why Miss Dove was the best teacher they could ever have.

'She never tells us off as strictly as Miss Sprout does.'

'Or shouts at us, like Mrs Moran does when she's had *enough*. Miss Dove would never, ever, *ever* lose her temper.'

'We are so *lucky*,' Beth reminded them all over again. 'We're lucky, lucky, *lucky* to have Miss Dove.'

And Philip just stayed very quiet.

2

'IS something wrong with your brains?'

That day it was really, really hot – far too hot to work. Miss Dove was starting a new project, all about travel. First, they made a list on the whiteboard of all the different ways there were of getting to other places. They'd called out all

the easy ones like planes and cars and trains and feet and bicycles and buses, but Miss Dove was still standing waiting.

She tried encouraging them. 'I know you can come up with a few more! Let's all try to think a bit more and a little harder. Come on, now. Who's going to be the first to think of another one?'

Still nobody spoke. A bee buzzed in the window and then buzzed out again. Sarah flopped on her desk and spread her arms to try to cool herself. Paul picked up his workbook and used it as a fan.

Miss Dove sighed. 'What is the *matter* with you all?' she said. 'Is something wrong with your brains today? Why aren't they working properly?'

'It's too hot,' Amari moaned.

'And too stuffy,' wailed Connor.

Astrid hated hot weather. It made her hands go sticky and her plaits feel heavy. So when Miss Dove told Connor and Amari, 'I don't see why the weather makes a difference. I don't see why you can't just *think*', Astrid said grumpily, 'You probably wouldn't like it if we did.'

Miss Dove turned from the whiteboard. Gently she smiled. 'Now you don't really believe that, do you, Astrid?'

'Maybe,' said Astrid. (She was in the mood to quarrel with anyone, even Miss Dove.) 'Maybe if we began to use our brains a lot, we would start arguing with you. I don't think you'd like that.'

Miss Dove beamed. 'Of course I wouldn't mind! It is my *job* to teach you how to think. So if you all began to think really hard about everything, I'd be delighted.' Miss Dove let out one of her merry, tinkling laughs. 'Why, Astrid, did you think I might get *cross*? Or lose my temper?'

'You might,' said Astrid.

'Only if we lived on Planet Fruitcake!'

'Perhaps we do,' said Astrid stubbornly.

3

On Planet Fruitcake

On Planet Fruitcake. Philip sat quietly, wondering what it meant. It sounded like some upside-down world in which teachers didn't want anyone to have ideas of their own, and people like him put up their hands in class and joined in the discussions.

It was a really strange idea. And he wasn't the only one to think so. Clearly Miss Dove did too, because she was saying, 'Of course we don't live on Planet Fruitcake! And I'm so sure we don't, I'll make a bet with you. You can all use your brains and think for a whole day, and if I once get cross or lose my temper, I'll buy the whole class a present.'

Everyone giggled at the very idea of sweet, kind, gentle Miss Dove losing her temper.

Except for Astrid. She just asked, 'What sort of present?'

'I haven't had time to think.' Miss Dove smiled. 'And you're not going to get one anyway. I'm going to win the bet because we don't live on Planet Fruitcake. No one does.'

Still, Philip thought, it was a nice idea. On Planet Fruitcake he'd be someone who put up his hand and joined in the discussions, just like everyone else.

Yes, Planet Fruitcake was the place to be.

4

An axe dripping with blood

'Right,' Miss Dove said encouragingly next morning. 'Ready to use your brains? Are all the tiny wheels inside your heads well-oiled and spinning nicely?'

Everyone nodded. It was cloudier today, and nowhere near so hot and stuffy. Everyone, even Astrid, felt ready to think.

'Good.' Miss Dove beamed. 'Then we'll begin the minute we get back from Assembly.'

But Philip started sooner than that. Because in Assembly Mrs Carter gave a little talk. 'Anyone can knock someone over in the playground by accident,' she said. 'But they should never try to put the blame on someone else. It's never, ever right to tell a lie.'

All the way back to the classroom, Philip was thinking. He knew that, if he lived on Planet Fruitcake, he would have something to say to the whole class. He'd put his hand up, just like all the others did.

Why not? Why couldn't he *pretend* he lived there. No one would know.

Before he could even think about it for one more minute, Philip had raised his hand.

Miss Dove stared.

So did everyone else.

Miss Dove said kindly, 'I see your hand's up, Philip. Have you left something in the hall you need to go back and fetch?'

'No,' Philip said. 'I wanted to tell you that what Mrs Carter just said to us – that it's never, ever right to tell a lie – well, that's plain *wrong*.'

Everyone stared even harder. Then Miss

Dove asked him gently, 'What makes you say that, Philip?'

He wasn't going to admit he only said it because he was pretending that he was on Planet Fruitcake. So he said, 'Because that's what I *think*.' And then, because they were still gazing at him in astonishment, he told them what he had been thinking all the way back from Assembly.

'Suppose you looked out of your window and saw a man waving an axe dripping with blood, and terrified people scuttling away up an alley. If he called up to ask you if you could see anyone trying to hide from him, it would be *right* to say you couldn't.'

'That's true!' Arif agreed. 'You'd say one tiny thing that wasn't true, but you'd save people's lives.'

They all chimed in. 'Yes. That's much more important.'

'What could be wrong with that?'

They sat and watched as Miss Dove had a quick think about it. In the end she said, 'Well, that's a *special* example.'

'Still,' Astrid said. 'It proves that Mrs Carter's wrong.'

5

Horribly dangerous

It seemed that most of the class agreed. 'Yes, it proves Mrs Carter's wrong.'

Miss Dove shook her head. 'No, I don't think so. Philip has given us a really good example, but you can't judge by only one.'

Philip sat quietly for a moment. But all the tiny wheels inside his head were well-oiled and spinning nicely. And he had another idea.

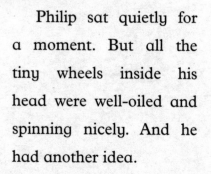

If he lived on Planet Fruitcake, he would put up his hand again to share it with the class. Why not?

Up went his hand again. 'Please, Miss Dove, I can think of another example. Suppose a boy runs into the street without looking, to try to catch his puppy, and gets knocked down. Then paramedics come in the ambulance, and tell him he has to keep absolutely still while they put a big plastic splint around his neck.'

'In case he's broken it?' asked Helen.

'That's right,' said Philip. 'But just as they're putting on the splint – terribly, terribly carefully – the boy asks if his puppy's all right. Well, I think, even if the paramedics didn't know, it would be better if they told him his pet was fine. At least till the splint was on.'

'Yes,' everyone agreed. 'That would be better.'

'Or else the boy would get upset and move his head about.' Tamara shuddered. 'That would be *horribly* dangerous.'

'Yes,' Paul agreed. 'So even if the paramedics actually *knew* that what they were saying was a lie, they should still say it.'

Philip looked round the class. He couldn't help feeling a little proud because it was obvious that everyone agreed with him, not with Miss Dove.

Miss Dove gave all of them a very vinegary look, the same way the janitor did when they tracked mud all over the clean floors. 'Oh, come on, class! Things like that aren't going to happen very often, are they?'

'Small children get run over all the time,' Tom pointed out. 'And lots of them must have been running into the road without looking, chasing their pets.'

'It could be happening right now, out on the street,' said Tamara.

Everyone swivelled in their seats to stare out of the window and check.

6

Deep in the jungle

You could tell that Miss Dove was pleased that Philip had put his hand up. Twice. But you could tell that she was also getting a little fed up with not being able to start the morning's work. She shook her head. 'Those are two very, *very* special cases.'

In his seat by the window, Philip had a third idea. Did he dare raise his hand again? Why not? He was on Planet Fruitcake, after all.

Up shot the hand. 'But I've thought of *another*. Suppose you were deep in the jungle with your best friend, and the two of you got separated. Suppose you thrashed through the undergrowth for days, totally lost. And then a tribe of local people found you. They looked a bit nasty-tempered, but they invited you to share their meal.'

Everyone gazed at Philip, thrilled by the story. They couldn't wait to hear more. And Philip suddenly realised that he was enjoying himself.

A lot.

He spread his hands. 'And it turned out that this tribe cooked their meals in one huge cooking pot. So you got on tiptoe to peer over the rim because you'd had no food for days, and you were really hungry.'

'Practically *starving*!' said Amari.

Philip took up his tale. 'The stew smelled good. But it was a bit grey and murky, and when you looked more carefully you saw your best friend's fingers and thumbs floating about on the top of it, all boiled up nicely.'

'Not *nicely*,' Tamara interrupted with a shudder. 'Please don't say boiled up *nicely*.'

'All right, then,' Philip agreed. 'But boiled up, and ready to be served with a nice banana dip.'

'He's doing it again,' Tamara complained to Miss Dove. 'He's saying "nicely" when it's just not *nice*.'

Philip ignored her. He turned back to Miss Dove. 'Well, if that happened, wouldn't it be *right* to tell a lie and say you were allergic to banana dip?'

'Or that eating boiled food was against your religion?' suggested Helen.

They all chimed in. 'Or that you just weren't hungry.'

'Any old lie, really.'

'Yes! Any old lie!'

'Rather than eat the cooked bits of your own best friend!'

Miss Dove pressed her lips tightly together,

25

rather the way Mrs Edmond did when she was getting ratty. 'That's all very well and good, class. And Philip's raised a really interesting point. But could we get back to work now, please?'

'I *knew* it!' Astrid crowed. 'I *knew* you wouldn't like it if we started thinking. I bet you're even starting to wish that we *did* live on Planet Fruitcake!'

Hastily, Miss Dove smiled. 'No, I am not,' she told Astrid firmly.

But sitting quietly again at his desk, enjoying everyone's looks of admiration, Philip had started to wish they did.

7

Something normal

'Was Astrid *right*?' Maria asked Miss Dove half an hour later, when they'd all finished their writing. 'Were you –'

She broke off. It didn't seem polite to ask a teacher if she was getting ratty, like Mrs Edmond sometimes did. So Maria put it another way. 'Were you a little bit fed up because we were trying to think?'

'No, no,' Miss Dove assured her. 'I am *delighted* that you're using your brains so well. It's just that those were all such very odd examples: mad axe-men, run-over children worrying about their pets, and jungle explorers kidnapped by cannibals. I don't think they really count. I think, for me to be convinced that Philip was right, he'd have to come up with something a little more *normal*.'

Everyone turned to Philip. It was obvious they were expecting him to think of something.

It felt very strange, everyone sitting there waiting for him to put up his hand. It really was as if they all were on a different planet.

He didn't want to let them down. So could he think of something?

Yes, he could.

Philip put up his hand. 'Suppose,' he said, 'that your really old neighbour was deciding what to do with her savings when she died. And suppose she planned to leave all her money to her gardener because he was always cheerful, and mended her fence whenever it blew over.'

'That's normal enough,' Tom told them all. 'Carry on, Philip.'

So Philip carried on. 'But suppose you knew her gardener was a terrible gambler and would lose all the money in only one day, betting on horses. But just as you were about to warn the old lady, she started gargling and choking, then dropped down dead.'

Jessica pushed back her chair and did a brilliant imitation of an old lady gargling and choking, then falling to the floor.

'Back on your seat please, dear!' said Miss Dove. She turned back to Philip with a slightly strained smile. 'Carry on, Philip.'

'So,' Philip said, 'when everyone came round to ask you what your old neighbour had wanted to do with her money, I think it would be better to say that she was planning to leave her savings to an orphanage, or a hospital.'

'Yes!' everyone agreed. 'That would be much more sensible.'

'No one would ever know.'

'It would be far, far better to tell a lie.'

Miss Dove sighed. 'All right. I do admit that Philip has thought of five very clever examples of –'

Without his even knowing it was going to

happen, Philip's hand shot up in the air again. 'Six!' he said. 'Because I've just thought of another. Suppose –'

'No, Philip!'

Everyone stared. For Miss Dove had said, 'No, Philip!' really sharply, exactly the same way Mr Huggett snapped at them when they were mucking about in the corridors. Astrid narrowed her eyes and peered more closely at Miss Dove's face. 'Please, Miss, you're not getting *cross*, are you?'

Miss Dove took a deep breath. 'Of course not!' she declared. She glanced at the clock. 'It's just that, however *wonderful* it is that all of you are using your brains so well, we don't have time to talk about this any more. It's nearly a quarter to ten, and time to get on with our board work!'

Astrid picked up her pencil. 'Well, all right,' she said. 'But when you see Mrs Carter in the staff room at break, you must promise to tell her that Philip has explained to us that what she told us in Assembly this morning was just plain *wrong*.'

'Yes,' everybody chorused. 'Just plain *wrong*.'

Weird and silly things

After break, they did maths. Miss Dove was asking questions round the class, and after a few minutes she reached Safira.

Safira couldn't answer. 'Sorry.' She blushed. 'I didn't hear what you said.'

'Because you weren't *listening*,' Miss Dove said. 'Because you were miles away, staring out of the window.' She smiled at Safira. 'Keep your dreaming for night-time, please, and then you won't be wasting time.'

At the next desk, Philip pricked up his ears. Whenever he was lying in bed and couldn't sleep, he thought about dreams. If things in the classroom were the same as usual, he wouldn't have said a word. But now that he was pretending that they'd all moved to Planet Fruitcake . . .

Philip put up his hand.

Miss Dove looked rather startled, as if she couldn't quite believe the change in him. One day he sat there, quiet as a mouse, and never joined in. The next, his hand was shooting up and down as often as a hotel lift.

But she'd been wanting him to join in the discussions, so all she said was, 'Yes, Philip? What do you want to say?'

'*I* thought,' said Philip, 'that maybe our night dreams *aren't* a waste of time. Maybe they are the *real* life that we have, and all this coming-to-school stuff in the daytime is really just in our dreams.'

Miss Dove said gently, 'I'm afraid that sounds a bit silly to me.'

Astrid was into the argument in a flash. 'I don't know. After all, in dreams at night you always think that you're awake. And yet you're not. So how can you be sure that, when you think you're awake in the day, you really are?'

Even Safira had stopped daydreaming now. 'That's right, Miss Dove! How do we know that all this going on around us isn't just a dream?'

Miss Dove said, 'If you were dreaming, you would realise as soon as you woke up.'

James told her cunningly, 'But I've dreamed in my dreams that I've just woken up. And that seemed *real*.'

'Yes,' Miss Dove said. 'But you can tell the difference because dreams are full of weird and silly things.'

Safira said stubbornly, 'But perhaps things really are the other way round. Maybe the *real* world's weird and funny, and dreams are simpler and more sensible. And *that's* why we think they're the real world.'

Miss Dove told them, a tiny bit impatiently, 'If this was not the real world, people would *know*.'

'How?' Astrid demanded.

'They just *would*.'

'But they could be *wrong*,' said Astrid. 'After all, you told us people used to think the sun went round the earth. And *they* were wrong.'

Judith said, 'And you told us that people used to think the world was flat, and if their boats sailed too close to the edge, they'd just fall off. But *they* were all wrong too.'

Safira was getting uppity now. 'Yes, they were wrong. But I bet they went round saying what Miss Dove said – that they just *knew* they were right.'

Behind her, Judith put on a cracked and wavery voice, pretending to be some ancient crone from olden times: 'It's *common sense*! You only have to look up to see the sun is going

round the earth, and not the other way round. And you only have to look around to see that, not counting hills and mountains, the world is flat.' She spread her hands and added in her normal voice, 'But they were all completely wrong.'

'Yes,' said Safira. 'Because they weren't really *thinking*.'

Astrid said slyly, 'Still, I bet their teachers were pleased with them, because they didn't keep interrupting lessons.'

Miss Dove's eyes suddenly went narrow as a cat's, and flashed the same scary way Miss Gelland's did when anyone forgot their sports stuff. And then, as if remembering that she was the nicest, kindest teacher in the whole school, she let out a little laugh. It wasn't her usual merry, tinkling laugh. In fact, it sounded rather as if it had been squeezed out of her throat with quite an effort. 'I know,' she said, 'let's talk about all this again when we have finished the lesson.'

Then she asked Tom the question she'd asked Safira at the start.

And since Tom hadn't been dreaming, either in this world or in any other, this time Miss Dove got an answer. And the answer was right.

9

Brains in pots

When she came down the steps into the playground at the end of break, Miss Dove was astonished to find her class in a circle round Philip, still talking about real and dream worlds.

'Ready to go inside?' she asked with a big smile. 'Where is my nice, straight, proper line?'

They shuffled into place. As they trooped through the swing doors, Sarah tugged at Miss Dove's sleeve. 'Miss Dove! Philip thinks maybe none of us is real *anywhere at all* – not in a dream *or* a real world.'

'Whichever is which,' Safira added.

41

'Yes,' Sarah said. 'Philip thinks maybe someone clever just invented us, and we're like creatures in a computer game.'

Miss Dove looked down at Philip. 'A *computer* game?'

This time he didn't even have to put up his hand. He only had to answer.

'Yes,' Philip said. 'One made by somebody so smart they've fooled us into thinking that our thoughts are our own.' He shrugged. 'We probably don't even have *bodies*, and are just brains in pots.'

Miss Dove raised an eyebrow. 'You think

we might just be *imagining* our bodies?'

'Yes,' Philip said. 'We might all be plugged into some amazing machine that sends messages along wires to our brains in pots to make us *think* that we can feel things like our skin and hair.'

They were all pitching in now. 'And makes us think that we can see things like our hands and fingers!'

'And our friends!'

'And all these wall displays along the corridor!'

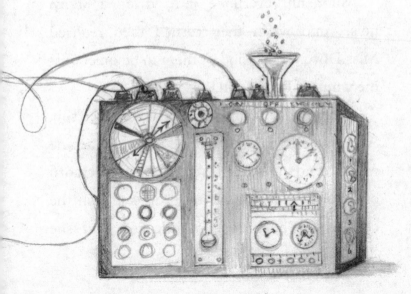

They were all calling out excitedly. 'Maybe this machine is *brilliant*, and makes us believe that we can hear things like the school buzzer!'

'And *taste* things – like the apple I just ate!'

Miss Dove laid a finger on her lips to make them all be quiet. But no one noticed because they had all turned to listen to Astrid, who was shouting from the back of the line, 'Maybe whoever put our brains in pots is so clever they even invented a way to make us think that we *remember* things, but really they just send our memories to us through a wire!'

Suddenly everyone jumped at a sharp noise, and when they turned they realised Miss Dove was hissing at them to be quiet, just the way Mr Pound did.

They all fell quiet as they heard her say, 'What *I* wish is that this really clever machine would send you all, right now, the memory of the rule that you have to talk softly in the corridors!' She'd gone a little red. But she

breathed deeply and then told them quietly, 'You are disturbing classes who have started work. Break time is over and I want you back inside the classroom now.'

'We can keep talking about it then, though, can't we?' persisted Astrid. 'I mean, you wouldn't want to stop us *thinking*, would you?'

Miss Dove gritted her teeth. 'Oh, no. That's the last thing I'd *ever* want to do. I'd never want to stop you *thinking*.'

10

Scoop out my brain

That's what she'd said – she'd never want to stop them thinking. And somehow, from the moment they were back in their seats, Philip found that he couldn't help it. All the tiny wheels inside his head were still spinning nicely, just the way she'd said she wanted them.

He couldn't help it. He put up his hand.

Miss Dove pretended that she hadn't seen.

Philip coughed politely.

Miss Dove pretended that she hadn't heard.

Astrid came to the rescue. 'Miss Dove! Miss Dove! Philip has had another thought!'

Miss Dove gave up. Sighing, she said, 'Yes, Philip?'

'What I *thought*,' said Philip, 'is that we can't be absolutely sure that *anybody's* brain really belongs to them.'

Miss Dove said as calmly as she could, 'I think we can, Philip, because our brains are safely inside our heads.'

'But doctors can do almost anything now,' said Philip. 'So how do I know for sure that someone didn't creep into my bedroom in the middle of the night, give me an injection so I didn't feel a thing, then very carefully scoop out my brain, and put it into someone *else's* head?'

Miss Dove said, 'Philip, I really do not think that we can waste any more class time talking about an idea as silly as this.'

'It isn't silly,' Astrid argued. 'It's *interesting*. I mean, after it happened, which person would be Philip?'

Miss Dove clapped a hand to her head.

'Astrid, it isn't going to *happen*!'

But Connor already thought he knew the answer. 'Philip would be the one who had Philip's body because we'd see him when he came through the gates next morning at school and we'd all say, "Hello, Philip!".'

'No,' said Safira. 'Philip would be the one who had Philip's *brain* put in his head, because Philip's brain has everything that Philip knows, and all his feelings and memories. And all that's *much* more important than what Philip looks like.'

'No, it's not,' said Connor. 'It has to be your *body* that counts. Because when you get up in the morning and look in the mirror, that's how you know it's *you*. And that's how your parents

know. And your friends. And your teacher.'

He looked at Miss Dove to see if she agreed. But it was impossible to tell whose side Miss Dove was on because Miss Dove was sitting with her head buried in her hands.

11

Married in a flowerpot hat

'Miss Dove?' Connor called gently. 'Miss Dove?'

But Miss Dove wouldn't look up.

They all sat quietly for a bit. But Philip couldn't stop thinking. And suddenly he found he couldn't bear it any more and, even without putting up his hand, he burst out, 'Connor, you are *wrong*. It can't be your body that matters most because people *change* so much.'

'Not that much,' Connor argued.

'Yes, they do! My great-granny has an album she keeps showing me whenever I go round. In it are photos of her when she was ten

days old. And you would *never* know that tiny baby was her. And there's a photo of her when she was our age, with big round eyes and pink cheeks. She's wearing a frilly apron frock and sitting on a rope swing. You wouldn't recognise her in that photo either. Then there's another one of her getting married in a flowerpot hat. And you would *still* not guess that she was my

great-granny. And there's –'
Miss Dove lifted her head and shot Philip quite a fierce look – exactly the same sort of look that Mrs Carter gave them when they whispered in Assembly.

Philip broke off.

'Thank you,' Miss Dove said. 'Thank you. Because we really must get down to work now.'

'Good!' Harry muttered in support. 'Because having to *look* at other people's family photos is boring enough. We don't want to *hear* about them.'

'That's not fair,' said Safira. 'And it's *rude*. Philip's not going on about his great-granny's photos for nothing. He's trying to explain that people keep looking different. And Philip's right.

Babies don't look a bit like anyone's great-grandmother, but they're the same person.'

Tom spoke up from the back. 'Yes, Philip's right. Because my dad knows someone who was in a gas explosion and his face got burned. He doesn't look at all like the person he was before, but my dad often meets him at the pub and always comes home saying, "He's the same old Jim".'

They all looked over to Miss Dove, but she had put her head back in her hands.

12

'Don't you *want* us thinking?'

Everyone waited politely. But when Miss Dove kept her face hidden, one or two of them decided they might as well carry on with what was turning out to be an interesting discussion.

'I've an idea,' said Beth. 'If you can't work out which person is really Philip – the one who has his brain or the one who has his body – maybe the thing to do is *ask*.'

'Ask which?' said Astrid.

'Both,' said Beth. 'Get the two of them together and ask, "Who thinks he's Philip?" then wait to see which of them answers.'

Harry was still feeling grumpy. 'I bet they *both* think they're Philip.'

Tasha said, 'Maybe neither of them does.'

'Maybe they'd be like us,' Philip suggested, 'and just not know.'

Miss Dove lifted her head to say irritably, 'Oh, Philip! How could you *possibly* not know if you were Philip or not.'

'I bet you could,' said Philip. 'But I'll have to *think* about it.'

Miss Dove lifted her head. 'Not now!' she warned him sharply. 'Not right now because we're going to get on with our work!'

'Why?' Astrid asked her. 'Don't you *want* us thinking?'

That was a big mistake. You could tell just from the look on Miss Dove's face. Everyone sat very still. The seconds ticked past on the clock. They all felt rather nervous.

Then Safira giggled. She couldn't help it. It was just the ticking of the clock, the look on

Miss Dove's face, and the stillness round her.

It was a *nervous* giggle. But it set them off. Soon they were all at it, giggling merrily.

Miss Dove rose to her feet and told them off as strictly as Miss Sprout did. First she reminded them that *she* was the teacher, not them. She pointed out that it was up to *her* to choose what they did in school time. And if she said that it was time to get back to work, then it was time to do *exactly that*.

She shook a finger at them. 'And no more giggling!'

They shook their heads. No. No more giggling.

And after that, all of them sat there very, very quietly, with no more giggling.

And got back to their work.

A clever and beautiful chicken

At lunch in the hall, Philip wouldn't let anyone sit by him. Each time someone set down their tray anywhere near, he said, 'Would you mind sitting somewhere else? I'm busy thinking.'

'You'll strain your brain,' warned Beth. But she still moved further along the table till she was sitting opposite Edward. She picked up her fork and poked at the dark red slice of something floppy on her plate. 'What's this?'

'The menu said that it was Chinese pork,' Edward informed her.

'Is it?' Beth's face dropped. 'Oh. I thought

60

it was that funny purple, shiny vegetable.'

'Do you mean aubergine?'

'I don't know what it's *called*,' said Beth. 'I only know I like it.' Skewering the floppy red slice with her fork, she flipped it neatly on to Edward's plate, saying, 'I don't think I like Chinese pork. *You* have it.'

Edward immediately flipped it back. 'I don't want it either. I don't eat meat.'

Beth asked him curiously. 'What, never?'

'No. I think it's wrong to eat animals.' He pointed his fork at her. 'After all, you wouldn't like to be eaten, would you?'

'No,' Beth admitted. 'But I'm a person, not an animal.'

'So? Animals might not want to be eaten either.'

'I'm sure they don't mind,' Beth argued. 'They're not going to worry about it, are they?

Because animals can't *think*.'

'Like Philip can?'

'Like Philip can.'

They shared a quiet chuckle. Then Edward said, 'But suppose they could. Suppose there was a really clever and beautiful chicken that grew up as someone's pet, and sat beside them while they learned to read, and learned to read as well. Suppose it listened to music too. And sometimes it paddled around in a paint box with wet feet, then walked on clean white paper to make beautiful pictures. And suppose it could count coins, and sat at that desk over there and took in the dinner money, and always got the change right. And suppose this chicken could understand jokes and, if you invited it to sit with you and told it something funny, it cackled with laughter.'

He pointed his fork at her again. 'Would you eat *that* chicken? Would you? Would you just cut off its head and pull out its feathers and shove it in an oven to *roast*?'

14

A really stupid baby

Beth had gone scarlet. 'What you just said is quite *ridiculous*,' she snapped. 'There's never been a chicken anywhere *near* that clever.'

'But if there *were*,' Edward persisted.

Beth had a think. Then she admitted, 'No. If I knew a chicken as bright and clever as that, I couldn't eat it.'

'But there have been an awful lot of stupid *people*,' Edward pointed out. 'So if not eating things is anything to do with them having good *brains*, then if you were hungry, you could find a really stupid person who –'

'Stop it!' Beth interrupted him.

'All right, then,' Edward teased her. 'Something less chewy? A baby! Suppose you came across a nice, juicy baby who couldn't walk or talk or even feed himself, and didn't know anything at all so, just like a chicken, he didn't mind the idea of being eat–'

'Be quiet!' Beth snapped. 'If you say another word about eating people or babies, I

will empty all these vegetables over your head.'

'All right, then,' Edward said. 'We'll stick with animals. What about your own cat? You're always telling us that Marmalade's not very bright. You told us she took three whole weeks to learn how to go through the cat flap. Would you eat Marmalade?'

Beth told him frostily, 'No one eats cats.'

'They *could*, though. After all, people in

other countries eat dogs. And donkeys. And horses.'

He smirked at her across the table. Beth attacked back. 'Well, *you* say that you won't eat animals because it's wrong. But wasting food's wrong too. So suppose a chicken in the road got hit by a car, but wasn't squashed. Then, if I cooked and ate it, I'd be doing something *useful*. But you would just leave it to rot, so you'd be wasting food.' She smirked back across the table. 'So I'd be being better than *you*.'

'You would not.'

'Yes, I would.'

'Would not!

'Would!'

Now they were really snarling at one another. Quite loudly. Everyone around stopped chatting so that they could hear what Edward and Beth were quarrelling about.

Up on the teachers' table, Mrs Carter turned to Miss Dove and said, 'See those two scrappers over there? Aren't they in *your* class?'

'Yes,' Miss Dove sighed. 'And the whole pack have been *impossible* today. The problem is, you know, they've started *thinking*.'

15

Suppose! Suppose! Suppose!

The moment Miss Dove came back into the classroom after the lunch break, Philip put up his hand. 'I've solved the problem, Miss Dove!'

'What problem?' asked Miss Dove.

'The one you asked me! How I could possibly not know if I was Philip or not!'

Miss Dove clenched her teeth. 'But you *are* Philip.'

'Yes. Yes, I am,' he said. 'But just *suppose* –'

Miss Dove groaned. 'Suppose! Suppose! That's all I've heard all morning! Suppose, suppose, suppose! We've hardly managed to do

70

a stroke of work because of all this supposing.' She gave the class a serious look. 'Now, I've a job to do and I'm afraid I must get on with it. I have to *teach* you.'

Astrid told her accusingly, 'But you said that it was your job to teach us how to *think*. And that's what Philip's doing.'

'Yes,' everyone chimed in. 'You said we *should* be thinking.'

'You said the only way you'd want us *not* to use our brains is if we lived on Planet Fruitcake.'

'And we *don't*.'

Hastily Philip lowered his head to try to hide the fact that he was going a bit pink. The rest of the class might be in the real world. But he was still pretending to be on Planet Fruitcake.

He didn't want the rest to guess. But they weren't looking his way. They were all gazing reproachfully at Miss Dove. 'You said you'd be *delighted* if we began to think.'

'You even made a bet that you wouldn't get cross.'

'I am *not* getting cross!' Miss Dove snapped. Then she forced a smile. 'All right, then, Philip. Come up to the front of the class, and try to explain to us how you might not know if you were you.'

16

The One and Only Philip

Philip had never been invited to stand out at the front of the class before. That only happened when someone had a lot to say in a discussion. Since it was awkward and uncomfortable to keep twisting round in your desk, so everyone could see and hear you easily, Miss Dove sometimes called people up to stand in her place to talk to the class.

He was a little nervous . . .

No! No, he wasn't, because he was on Planet Fruitcake!

Philip stood tall and straight. '*Suppose*,' he

said, 'that I was a boat.' He spread his arms. 'A huge, enormous boat. And I was called *The One and Only Philip*, and had a name plate made for me and fixed on the side.'

'Funny name for a boat,' Beth muttered.

Philip ignored her. 'And suppose one day, in a bad storm, my mast snapped off and fell into the sea and floated out of sight.'

'You'd need a new one,' Harry pointed out.

'Yes. So suppose my owners got one exactly the same, and fitted it on. And then there was another storm, and this time all my sails were whipped away. And so my owners had more made.'

'Exactly the same?'

'That's right. And then the name plate on my side fell off and so –'

Everyone interrupted him to chorus, 'Your owners had another made, exactly the same!'

'Yes. Then let's pretend we went out sailing every weekend. And just about every time we did, my owners noticed that one or another of the planks in me was going rotten. So they'd prise it out and chuck it overboard and fit in a new one.'

'Just the same!'

'Yes. Just the same. And over the years, one by one, every single plank I had got thrown

out and replaced. So I became a whole new boat. But because it happened so slowly and gradually, all of us still thought of me as *The One and Only Philip*.' He grinned. 'But *suppose* –'

Behind him, he thought he heard a tiny groan from Miss Dove. But he ignored it. '*Suppose* it just so happened that my old mast, and all my blown-away sails, and my boat's rusty name plate, and all the planks my owners had thrown out, happened to float away on the same ocean current. So one by one they had all ended up on the same island.'

They were all gazing at Philip now, enchanted by the story.

'And on this island was a sailor who had been marooned for years.'

'What's *marooned*?' asked Safira.

'Stuck.' Philip told her. 'Can't get off. But this sailor could make boats. So he used all the old bits that floated to his shore to make a boat

of his own so he could escape. It took him years, but in the end he'd fitted them together. And it just so happened that he put them all in exactly the same places as they had been before. So, by the time he'd finished, the boat he'd made just happened to look –'

'Exactly the same!' they chorused.

'Yes, exactly the same! Then he went sailing off. And just by chance he sailed past me and my owners.' Philip grinned. 'Two ships! But we can't *both* be *The One and Only Philip*, can we?'

He turned to face Miss Dove in triumph. '*See?*'

17

'I will not have this pandemonium in my classroom!'

Instantly, everyone started arguing.

'Well, you're the *first* one, aren't you? You are the boat the sailor built from all the old stuff. Because that's what you were made from first.'

'No, you're your owners' *new* one. Even though you only turned into it gradually.'

'I don't think you're *either*. If there are *two* of you, how can either of you be *The One and Only*?'

'I think they're *both* you.'

'No, that can't be right. *The One and Only Philip* can't be two boats at once! That's stupid!'

'And impossible!'

'Then it's the first.'

'No, the second!'

Miss Dove strode to the window. She faced the street outside. Those of the class who sat nearby said afterwards that they had heard her counting, very slowly, up to ten under her breath. But even when she'd finished, most of the class were still arguing fiercely.

'It has to be the *new* boat! Along with the owners that he had before!'

'No, it's the one made out of all the old bits, because that's more like what it was when it began.'

'I don't think that it's either of them now!'

'Well, I still think it's both!'

Miss Dove spun round. 'Be quiet!' she shouted, just the way Mrs Moran always shouted at them when she'd had *enough*. 'Everyone be quiet! Right now! I will not hear another word! I will not have this pandemonium in my classroom. All of you be quiet! *Now!*'

Everyone fell silent, and it was quite a while before Safira dared lean closer to Astrid and whisper, 'What's pandemonium?'

'Noise,' Astrid whispered back. 'Chaos and noise, like lots of devils fighting.'

Then they both sat up straight and stared towards the front. And, as he walked past on the way back to his seat, Philip heard Astrid muttering sourly under her breath.

'I *warned* her,' she was grumbling. 'I *knew* that she would get upset. I told her at the start that she'd be much, much happier away from Planet Fruitcake, with nobody *thinking*.'

18

Purple cows and black ice lollies

To try to distract them, Miss Dove let everyone do art. Paul and Maria handed round the tubs of poster paints. Prue reached up. 'Can I have that red, please?'

Paul held out one of the pots.

'No,' Prue said. 'The one behind. It's a better red and I'm going to paint a fire.'

'They're all the same red,' Paul pointed out. 'Poured from the same bottle.'

'Well, that one in the back looks redder to me.'

'Then you must have different eyes from

everyone else.'

'Maybe she has,' said Philip. Without even bothering to pretend he was on Planet Fruitcake, he raised his hand. 'Miss Dove, how do we know that Prue is seeing the same red as everyone else?'

Miss Dove suggested hopefully, 'Because she can see it?'

'But how do we know she's seeing the same as we see?' He waved his paint brush in the air. 'It could be that she sees her colours differently from everyone else.'

'I think she'd know by now if she were colour blind.'

'No. I don't mean she might be colour blind. I mean she might just see things *differently*.'

Prue grinned. 'Yes! Maybe when I look at yellow, what I see is *grey*. I call it yellow because, since I was a baby, every single time I saw something that looked grey to me, someone else called it yellow. So I learned the words wrong and I think that grey means yellow.'

Miss Dove told her faintly, 'Prue, I'm quite sure you see exactly the same colours we all see.'

Prue argued, 'But you don't *know*. Not unless you climb into my brain with a paint chart, and hold it up against what I have at the back of my eyes when I say I see yellow, and check it's the same as what you see, and what's called yellow on the paint chart.'

Miss Dove said, 'I wouldn't have to climb inside your brain. I could just hand the paint chart round and tell you all to point to yellow to check you all pick the same colour.'

'Yes,' Philip argued. 'But she might still be seeing *grey*. Maybe I see red sky, but just because the whole world goes round saying the sky is blue, I think that colour must be blue.'

They were all interested now. 'Then maybe you see purple cows.'

'Maybe I see black ice lollies.'

'Or green toast.'

'Or pink leaves.'

Miss Dove raised her hand for quiet. Nobody even noticed. They just kept on shouting out.

'Or lavender bread.'

'Or orange water.'

'Or snow-white chimneys.'

Miss Dove tried to interrupt. 'Everyone,

please! I know you're usually allowed to talk while we're doing art. But you're all getting far too excited and –'

'Or blue salad!'

'Or a grey sun!'

'Or –'

'– *far* too noisy –'

'Or violet blood!'

'Black milk!'

'– and I want you to stop calling out –'

'Silver mud!'

'Cream ink!'

'– at once! Just stop it! All of you! Right now! Right now! Do you hear me, class? You're to shut up! Every last one of you! This moment! Shut up!

Shut up!

Shut up!'

19

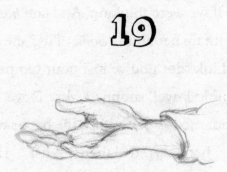

You've Lost the bet

Everyone stared. Angry red patches gleamed on Miss Dove's cheeks. Her eyes were sharp and bright. Her fingers were as stiff as claws. She looked quite frightening.

All of the people who'd been out of their seats crept back to their places. Everyone else hastily picked up their paint brushes so they could try to pretend that they'd been working quietly the whole time.

There was a very long silence. Finally, Safira nudged Astrid. 'Go on, then. Tell her that she lost the bet. She said she wouldn't lose her temper if we were thinking. And she *has*.'

Astrid put up her hand. '*Some* of us,' she said tactfully, 'think that you've lost your temper.'

'I certainly have!' snapped Miss Dove.

'And that means you've lost the bet as well.'

'What bet?' And then Miss Dove remembered. 'Oh!'

'Yes,' Astrid said. 'And now that you've got cross because we were all thinking, you have to buy the class a present.'

Miss Dove took a deep breath. Gradually the red spots on her face began to fade.

'Oh, dear,' she said. 'Well, I suppose I do.'

20

The most suitable present

Next morning, when they all trooped into class, there was the most enormous golden box on Miss Dove's table. It had rainbow ribbons round it, and a huge floppy bow.

'Is that our present?' asked Sarah.

'It certainly is,' said Miss Dove.

All of them gathered around it, chattering excitedly.

'What's in there, Miss Dove?'

'That box is *huge*.'

'I love those ribbons.'

'Can we open it *now*?'

'Break time,' said Miss Dove.

They worked all morning. Most of them were tired from all the thinking on the day before, and just got on with their work. Once or twice, Philip lifted his hand and said, '*Suppose –*' but everyone quickly hushed him.

At break time Miss Dove told everyone that they could open the box. Sarah pulled off the ribbon, and Arif lifted the cardboard flaps and peeped inside.

'Cake! It's the biggest cake I've ever seen!'

They all peered in.

'It's covered in icing!'

'And as big as a *planet*!'

'What sort of cake is it?'

'Guess!' Miss Dove said. 'Since it turns out we seem to live there.'

'It's *fruitcake*!' they all shouted. And it was delicious. But Philip had two extra presents of his own, because the next time his parents came into school, Miss Dove told them that Philip

joined in really well whenever they were talking about things in class.

And when he got his next report, he saw that she had written:

*In class discussions, Philip is **excellent**! I'm **very** pleased.*

Starting a Story

Write your own story about a strange day at school. If you can't think of a way to start, try one of these:

a) It took me a while to realise what was so wrong that morning. No one was speaking. No one.

b) We were only five minutes into the lesson when it suddenly landed on the playground outside the window. I'd never seen anything like it.

c) 'Quick!' Pip warned. 'I hear Mrs Brown coming!' But when door opened, what/who should we see but . . .

Anne's Top Tips for Writing

1. If you don't get started, you'll never finish.

2. Write the story that you yourself would most like to read but no one has bothered to write for you.

3. Keep your story hidden unless you feel like sharing. Some people enjoy talking to others about what they're doing. Some people don't. Do whatever works for you.

4. Don't take on too much. Stories get complicated very fast, so stick with a fairly simple idea and develop it well.

5. Don't just tell us what happened next, over and over, like a cartoon. Explain what your characters are thinking and feeling and worrying about. Believe it or not, that's far more interesting for a reader than things like car chases and fights, which work so much better on screen.

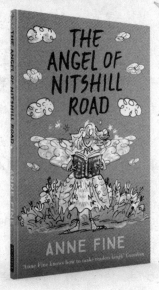

'Anne Fine is an author who knows how to make readers laugh'
The Guardian

Read all of Anne Fine's hilarious stories of classroom chaos